Who's Hiding?

First published in Japan in 1993 by Poplar Publishing Co, Ltd
English language edition published by arrangement by Kane/Miller Book Publishers, Inc

This edition first published in Australia and New Zealand in 2008 by Gecko Press
PO Box 9335, Marion Square, Wellington 6141, New Zealand
Email: info@geckopress.com
Reprinted 2009, 2010

National Library of New Zealand Cataloguing-in-Publication Data
Onishi, Satoru.
Asonde asonde. English
Who's hiding? / Satoru Onishi.
ISBN 978-1-87746-712-7 (hbk)
ISBN 978-1-87746-713-4 (pbk.)
[1. Animals—Fiction. 2. Questions and answers. 3. Visual perception.] I. Title.
895.65—dc 22

Typesetting: Beetroot Communications Ltd
Printing: Everbest, China

ISBN paperback: 978-1-877467-13-4
ISBN hardback: 978-1-877467-12-7

For more curiously good books, visit www.geckopress.com

Who's Hiding?

Satoru Onishi

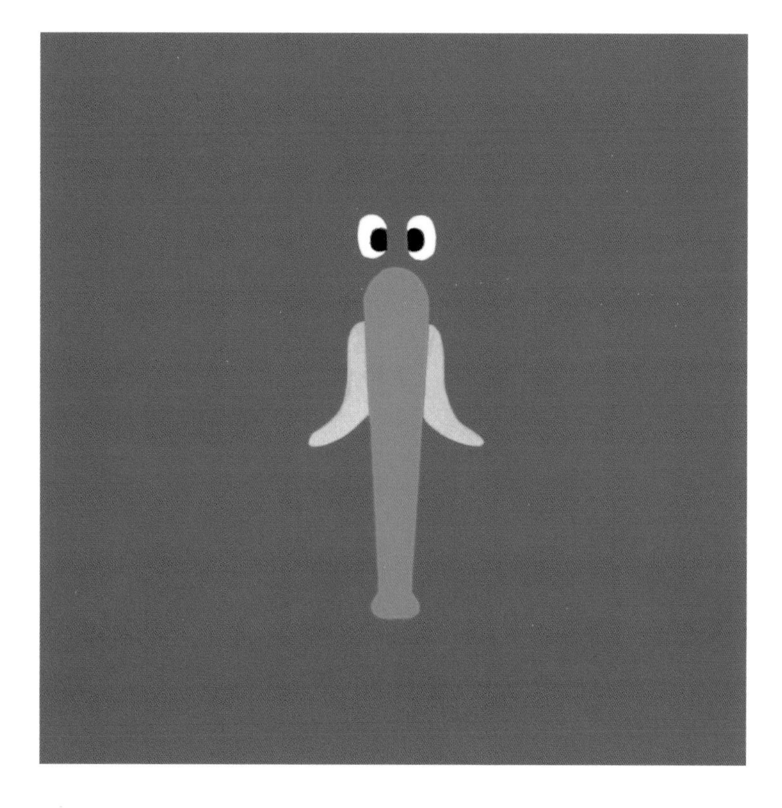

GECKO PRESS

Dog

Tiger

Hippo

Kangaroo

Lion

Rabbit

Rhino

Pig

Sheep

Zebra
Bear
Reindeer
Giraffe
Monkey
Bull
Hen
Elephant
Cat

Who's hiding?

Who's crying?

Who's hiding?

Who's angry?

Who's hiding?

Who has horns?

Who's hiding?

Who's backwards?

Who’s hiding?

Who's sleeping?

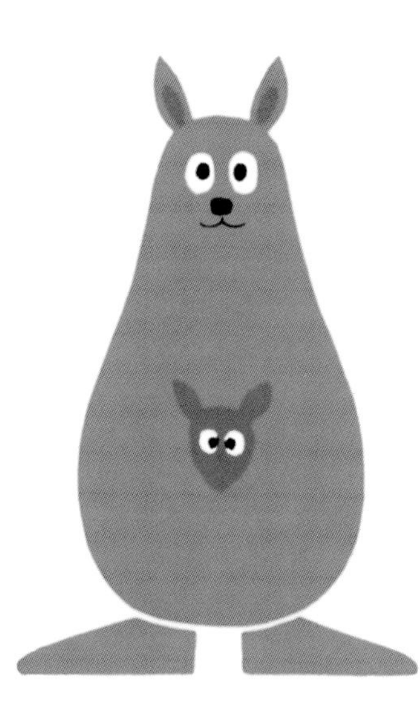

Who's hiding?

Who's backwards?

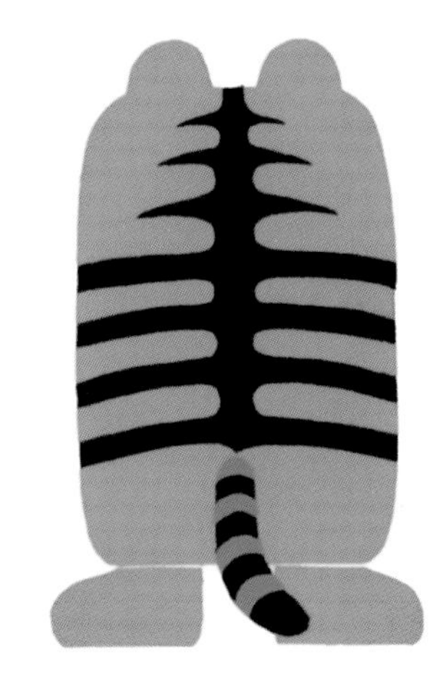

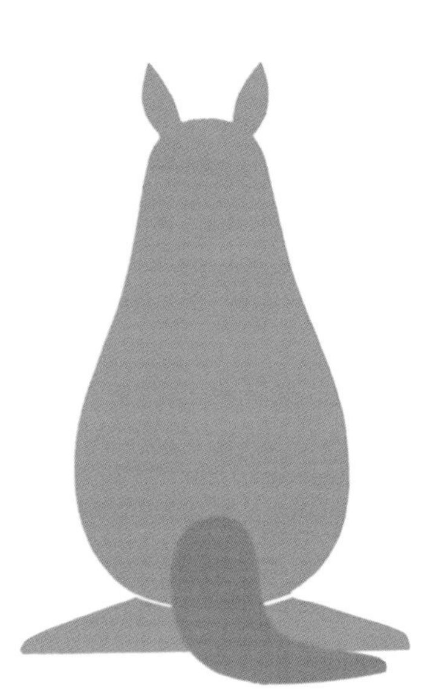

Who's who?

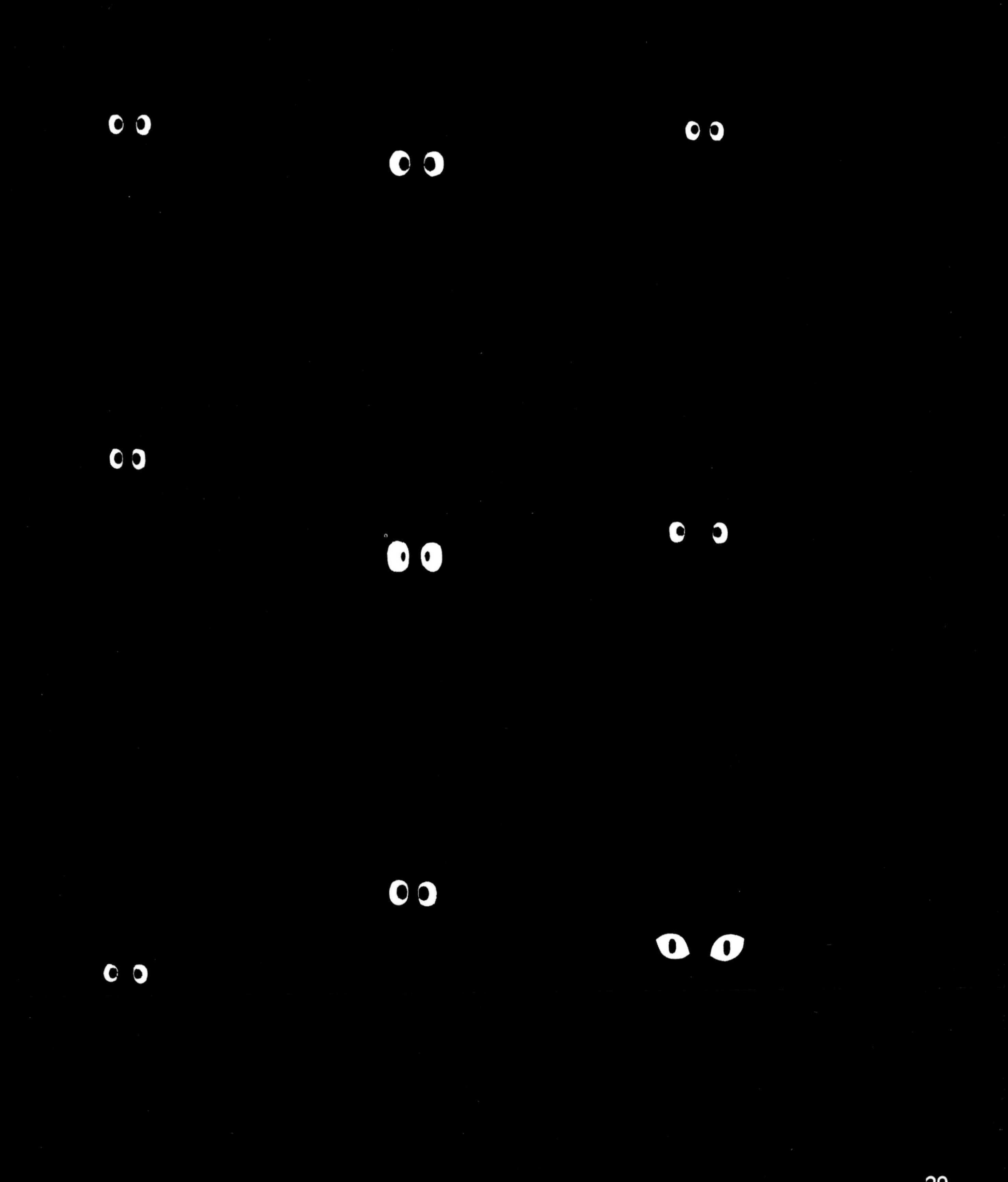

Dog

Tiger

Hippo

Kangaroo

Lion

Rabbit

Rhino

Pig

Sheep

Zebra
Bear
Reindeer
Giraffe
Monkey
Bull
Hen
Elephant
Cat

Answer Key

Pages 4–5	Reindeer is hiding.
Pages 6–7	Rabbit is crying.
Pages 8–9	Hippo is hiding.
Pages 10–11	Bear is angry.
Pages 12–13	Giraffe, Rhino, and Cat are hiding.
Pages 14–15	Reindeer, Giraffe, Bull, Rhino, and Sheep have horns.
Pages 16–17	Dog, Lion, and Monkey are hiding.

Pages 18–19	Pig is backwards.
Pages 20–21	Bear, Rabbit, Pig, and Elephant are hiding.
Pages 22–23	Rhino is sleeping.
Pages 24–25	Tiger, Zebra, Kangaroo, Bull, Sheep, and Hen are hiding.
Pages 26–27	Tiger, Bear, Kangaroo, Lion, Monkey, Hen, and Cat are backwards.
Pages 28–29	Dog, Tiger, Hippo, Zebra, Bear, Reindeer, Kangaroo, Lion, Rabbit, Giraffe, Monkey, Bull, Rhino, Pig, Sheep, Hen, Elephant, Cat